I0631306

Latham Cornell Strong

Midsummer dreams

Latham Cornell Strong

Midsummer dreams

ISBN/EAN: 9783743383456

Manufactured in Europe, USA, Canada, Australia, Japa

Cover: Foto ©Andreas Hilbeck / pixelio.de

Manufactured and distributed by brebook publishing software (www.brebook.com)

Latham Cornell Strong

Midsummer dreams

MIDSUMMER DREAMS

BY

LATHAM C. STRONG

AUTHOR OF "CASTLE WINDOWS," AND "POKE O' MOONSHINE."

NEW YORK

G. P. PUTNAM'S SONS

182 FIFTH AVENUE

1879.

Copyright by

G. P. PUTNAM'S SONS.

' 1879.

TO

MY MOTHER

WITH FILIAL REVERENCE, FOND AFFECTION,

AND TENDER MEMORIES.

CONTENTS.

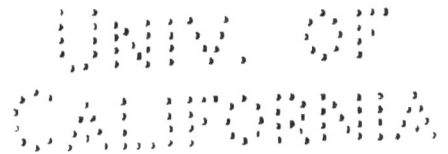
UNIV. OF
CALIFORNIA

MIDSUMMER DREAMS

FLORETTE.

THEY know my heroine was fair
   Because such memories do cling
And leave their impress everywhere
About the place of which I sing.—
Shadow and sunshine on the wall
Are flickering, fading, waving low,
Sunset-castles aflame, and all
The green sea-waters in a glow !
O bonnie birds ye sang so sweet
Down by the breeze-blown yellow wheat,
And by the brook, where tinkling bells,
And silver flutings down the dells,
Were blending in such merry chime
Through all that golden summer-time !

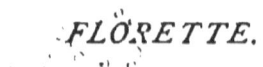

FLORETTE.

A path led sea-ward from the dell,
And from the little cottage old,
Where dwelt Florette, with close, and fold
Of poplar tree, and trough, and well
Of bubbling water trickling down
Gray sand-stone ledges to the lane
That wound to yonder sea-port town.
And round the house at sight of rain,
How seemed the flowers to scamper so,
Each one a little prince or nun—
And then at times to curt'sy low
With shy hid faces, in the sun !
And o'er the porch in silken sheen,
The vine-leaves hung and swung a maze,
In mellow shades of gold and green
Aslant the floor those summer days !

She's sleeping well—my poor Florette—
Alas, the little maid was blind !
Scarce seven summers when we met
Had bowed their roses in the wind,
Or filled the violets with dew.

Scarce seven summers old, and you
Would have so loved her airy grace,
Her gentle heart, and winsome face !

'Twas here we sat in days of rest,
I, curate of a parish old—
And she, poor lassie, striving best
To understand the tales I told
Of how the singing-birds do come
And build their homes in summer trees,
And why around the flowers hum
The drowsy-droning yellow bees.
Of how the nightingale doth sing
By moonlight in the quiet dell,
Of seed-time, and of harvesting,
And what the lonely petrels tell
When skimming o'er the billow's crest,
And gray and gloomy grows the west.
But most she loved to hear the tales
From Scripture, and in holy eves
Would walk with me through quiet vales
And listen midst the warm green leaves

To Jacob's Dream of angels bright,
Star-browed, and lightly floating down
The ladder in the dazzling light
Of snow-white wings, and shining crown ;
Or of the child who sagely talked
With wisdom more than man's can be ;
Or of the Holy One who walked
Upon the waves of Galilee.
And so through many a pleasant day,
We strolled together hand in hand,
And sailed upon the sunny bay,
Or wandered down the firm beach sand.

And are you sleeping gently yet ?—
Or do you see the kingdom bright,
The lily and the rose, Florette,
And white doves flying in the light ?
The violet trembles on thy grave
And hides its face in sun or rain,
The birds return across the wave
And sing of thee in plaintive strain !

Aye—she was timid of the sea,
When it upheld its voice of wrath,
And shrieked, and hurled defiantly,
Its strength across her sea-side path.
And of the wind when overhead
The summer thunders rolled across,
That seemed to her like legions led
By Satan, groaning o'er their loss.
But ev'ry morn, come sun or rain,
With dear old Gerald sitting there,
(*Poor fellow! in his grief and pain,*
He seldom speaks for sheer despair—)
Florette would seek her brother's mill
Across the sands and pasture grass
Where high-tide waters rush and fill
The meadow-lands, and wild morass,
To bring each day his noontime fare.
(*Nay Gerald, courage, strive to feel*
That she can see now over there !)
And every morn with gentle face,
She used to pass my gate and say
Some pleasant word with winning grace,

And wait a kiss, and trip away
Tugging at Gerald's gaberdine,
Across the salt-sea meadows green.
And so it was, in cloud or sun,
Each morn along the reaching sand,
Out from the town of Templeton,
They went together hand in hand.

One eve—it seems as if she knew
The sorrow of that dreadful day—
When skies were all aglow, we two
Strolled down the beach of yonder **bay**
Where lay a yawl upon the dune ;
And sitting in the rising moon,
She clasped her hands upon my knee,
And turned a pale, sad face, and told,
Softly, while o'er the summer sea
The music of the waters rolled,
Her dream of doves so seeming bright,
Like snow, she thought, that round her flew ;
And how there came a strange white light
That, floating downward through the blue,

Approached her, when she saw, amazed,
A crown that brightly burned and blazed,
With all the glory of the sky.
" And do the angels wear a crown,
And will I see them when I die ?
Oh, often when I'm lying down,
And night has come, as people say,
And all is dark the same as day,
Around me angel faces seem
Like those, you know, in Jacob's dream—
But last night one stood waiting long
With lifted hand, and smiling gaze,
While far away I heard the song
They sing in church on Sabbath days ! "
(*And Gerald, in her evening prayer,*
She prayed that you might meet her there
Beyond the silence where the skies
Make bright the shores of Paradise.)

Then came a day of parching heat,
The very sea its cry forgot,
The gray sands glimmered at my feet,

And all the air was still and hot.
Florette had started for the mill
Some time before, and up the hill
Across the downs I faint recall
Two fading forms, and that is all.
Then to the rectory I turned
While all the sky bright yellow burned,
Save one long line of gray and brown
That lay along the western sea ;
And wearily I laid me down
And slumbered, tossing restlessly.

I woke to feel the cold air sweep
Across me through the open door—
I rose, and looked upon the deep
To hear the wild winds rage, and roar,
And all the meadows blind with rain.
And then there came a crackling sound,
And wild against the window-pane,
The tempest beat its baffled wings,
And once I thought I heard a cry
Afar off, but it ceased, and then

It faintly seemed to come again ;
While deeply rolled across the sky
The tempest's awful mutterings.
I closed the door—and darker came
The clouds, white-edged, beyond the trees,
And then a blinding, crashing flame
Rang down the level of the seas
That surged like weird shapes up the hill !
I thought of her—my poor Florette—
With Gerald waiting at the mill,
And safely housed from wind and wet,
When once again a cry of pain—
Then sound of voices far below—
And from the window through the rain,
I saw men running to and fro
Beside the flooded meadow-lands.
And some were leaning o'er the sands—
And then I thought of poor Florette,
And dashing madly through the door,
Down where the gathering crowd had met,
I found her dead upon the shore !

Gerald was there—but she had died—
And he lay senseless at her side.
Alas her fate !—the strongest arm
Could not have borne her safe from harm
In that wild flood.—

They laid her where
The Sabbath music thrills the air,
Where daisies white grow wild and free—
In yonder churchyard by the sea.

THE LITTLE LADY IN WHITE.

HE sun is out, and the rain is over,
The streets are bright with a flood of gold,
And fancies born of the swinging clover
Come up again as they came of old.

In tall tree-towers the birds are singing,
Burdened and bowed are the fields of grain,
Softly the village bells are ringing,
Slowly the cows come up the lane.

Under the garden-hedge the spider
Crosses his bridge with its rain-drop lamps,
The beetle falls where the path grows wider,
Prone on his back in the web-spun camps.

A mellow glow through the forest clearing—
Sinking now is the sun to rest—
Like a silver boat in the blue is nearing
Slowly the new moon towards the west.

By the open window to-night is lying
My little lady robed in white,
And she lifts a pale, sad face, and sighing,
Longs to roam in the meadows bright.

Black bats whir in the white-rose garden,
Crickets chant in the meadows nigh,
The owl from its oak like a watchful warden,
Stares at the star in the southern sky.

Tinkle of bells in the rocky ledges !
Tumbling the waters flash and flow—
The frogs are out in the swamps and sedges,
The watch-dog's bark sounds far and low.

Fast asleep on her pillow dreaming,
Angel-voices she seems to hear
And snow-white wings in the starlight gleaming,
Flash through a glistening atmosphere.

Now she skips over golden meadows,
Tossing her curls in the fragrant air,
And behind the crystal rocks like shadows
Hover the pixies here and there.

Up in a mountain a bright throng listens
Unto the song to the rising moon,
Over the waters a city glistens
Like diamond skies of an eve in June

My little white-robed lady surely
Fears not sprite, or bright-winged fay,
With finger upon her lip demurely,
Still she stands where the pixies play.

Often she gazes across the waters,
Fretted with silver, and edged with gold,
Often she watches the sea-bright daughters
Walking so still in the waters cold.

Alas, at her side in hat and feather,
In lace and satin and pointed shoon,—
His milk-white steed is pawing the heather—
She sees the Erl-king against the moon !

He tells of a beautiful land of flowers,
Of children that stroll by the shining sea,
Of streets of pearl, and of twinkling towers,
And birds that sing in the bended tree.

He lifts her up on the steed that bore him—
My little lady robed in white—
And over the rippling waves before him,
Dashes away through the dreamy night.

Over the twinkling reach of waters,
Gallops the steed with my lady fair,
Below in the depths are the sea-bright daughters
With outstretched arms and with streaming hair.

White are the walls of the city yonder,
Fair as the realm of the morning star,
And she lifts her eyes with a look of wonder,
And voices of old sound faint and far.

And a clear blue light on her path is falling,
And all the gates swing wide and free,
But ever she lists to her loved ones calling
Sadly over the silent sea !

———

Morning breaks through the croft of beeches,
The pansy pushes its hood aside,
And peeps at the sun, and across the reaches
Of meadow, the winding waters glide.

But the birds sing low with hearts forsaken,
The roses are bowed with a weary pain,
For my lady in white will never awaken,
Nor over the waters return again !

REMEMBRANCE.

GONE are the guests from the banquet hall,
  And the music of harp and flute
That thrilled the heart of the passionate rose
  In the garden, is hushed and mute.
The moonlight falls on the velvet floor,
  And the wax-light glare is fled,
But I see in the bloom of the violet light,
  The ghosts of the buried dead.

The marble statues in purple seem
  To shine through a tremulous mist,
And the chandeliers like diamonds change
  To rose, and to amethyst.
And phantoms come in the dreamy glow,
  And pass me with tender grace,
With averted head, and with tearful eyes,
  But at times with a lifted face.

One by one through the arches dim,
  They glide to the open door,
And fade away where the moonlight falls
  On the crimson-velvet floor.
And I lean in the shade of the ilex here,
  With a heart that is filled with woe,
For I know they are memories pale and sad
  Of the silent long ago !

THE CHILDREN OF ROXBURGHSHIRE.

PROUD heart had Sir Wallace Vaughn,
 The sturdiest clansman of all his peers ;
Full seventy summers had come and gone,
And now he had reached the twilight-years.
Into his deep-stained windows came
The purple and orange of sunset flame
In a shaft of light on the oaken floor ;
And he sat in his quaint old Gothic room
Half in color, and half in gloom,
With his deer-hound dozing beside the door.
And what cared he for court or crown,
From his castle-turrets his bonnie flag
With its Wallace plaid looked bravely down
Over Cheviot moor, and Eildon crag,
And shook a menace like mailéd hands
In the golden breeze to the border lands !
And poor old Margery bowed with age,

With the castle-keys at her apron belt,
What cared she for serf or page,
Or how the equerry-in-waiting felt,
As she mumbled her orders and hobbled away
From the room of her master old and gray,
Like herself, but still at seventy year
The chief of his clan in Roxburghshire !

Twilight crept through the lonely hall,
And the battered shield on the gloomy wall,
The crossed swords over the carven door,
The tall gold vases with silver wings,
And the elk-skin mat on the polished floor
Changed slowly to weird and eldritch things.
Then the old man rose as the stars looked in,
And he opened the door to the owlet-glow
Of the single sconce, and the merry din
Of the horse-boy's song in the courts below.
And he leaned him against the window bars,
And he bent his gaze on the twilight stars,
Till the moon came up above the brae,
Till he saw emerge from the forest dark

A monk from the Abbey of Achray,
And cross the courtyard through the park.
Up the wide winding stairs he came,
While Margery bustled through the gloom
Till the tapers burned with a snow-white flame,
Throughout that ancient Gothic room.

And now the twain together stood—
The monk in his hermit gown and hood,
With folded arms, and with bended head,
Pondered the words that the old chief said,
As he led his guest in the ancient hall
With its triple candelabra tall,
And its knights in armor looking down
With their steel teeth set in a sullen frown.

"You have heard;"—he said—"how peaceful toil
Thrives but too well on Scotland's soil
At a time when men in deadly fray
May meet at the pibroch's sudden call.—
At sight of their little bairns at play,
At woman's tears, and childhood's thrall,
Listless they bide with unnerved hand,

The buffet of a brave man's brand.
As close as bees in the clover new,
As wild as the birds about my door,
That chatter and chirp the long day through,
That screech and call over heath and moor
And swarm in the vines of the castle wall,
And hover about the brake and mere,
Are the bairns of my clansmen about my hall,
And throughout the braes of Roxburghshire.
For this I called you to meet me here,
That you herald my mandate near and far,
By Hawick town, and by flowing Tweed,   .
Wherever my thrifty clansmen are,
That every mither and bairn proceed
To the far-off fortress of Achray,
Nor again set foot on fell or crag,
Wherever floats the Wallace flag
Till such a season as I shall say ! "

About his castle in Roxburghshire
The ivy had crept for many a year,
And many an oak in the park had grown
So huge that its age was scarcely known.
And around the castle the children played,
And thousands of birds flew out and in
Through leafy courts in the tremulous shade
Where the sun-gold weavers sit and spin.

The throstle, the jay, and the mavis brood
Swarmed in the vines, or swung in flight
In a wave of melody through the wood,
Where the children romped through the gowan white.
The wrens looked out from their peeping nests,
The robins folded their wings and sat
On the castle towers in garrulous chat
With the templar mark on their ruffled breasts—

And bevies of black-birds about the ground
In circle would stand for hours sedate,
Like cowled inquisitors around
Their leader discussing affairs of state.
And the bullfinch after a few sweet words,
Would bow to his fellows on either side,
And squawk his contempt of other birds
Puffed up with their bold conceit and pride.
And through the meadows the bairns would stray,
With rosy cheeks and with flaxen hair,
Skipping and tripping here and there,
And their feathered friends would join in play,
And feed from their hands without a fear—
So tame were the birds of Roxburghshire !

The banners drooped in the evening breeze,
The moon shone clear, through the summer trees,
Across the park with its satin sheen
Of poplar groves on the village green.
And the little ones were gathered all
At the children's May-night festival.
In plume and plaid neath the silver glow

The winsome shapes moved to and fro,
And never did moonlight forest ring
From Teviot's scaurs to the braes of Tyne,
With the bonnie cheer of such gathering
Since Llynarch sang in days lang syne.
Lassies with golden curls and fair
As fairies that sing on the Caldon Low,
With eyes as bright as the throssle's are,
Danced to the merry music's flow.
And lads like the craggie sprites that toss
Their caps in the rocks of the eerie folks
Laughingly ran in their glee across
The wide white spaces between the oaks.—
But above at the castle a form looked down
At the moonlight scene with a face a-frown ;
And it muttered a curse as it turned away
From the window, at sight of the bairns at play.
And in dreams that night, Sir Wallace saw
The foemen swarming by hill and glen,
And he sprang to the midst of the fight again
Where amid his clansmen his word was law.
But his feet were bound and his arm was stayed,

And in vain he lifted his trusty blade,
For about him were children by hundreds massed,
Who tugged at his kilt, and who held him fast.
Then he struck them down in their places dead,
Till his strength was gone, and his hands were red,
And their death-cries rang in his startled ear
As the morning broke over Roxburghshire !

But a sad procession set out that day
To the convent prison of old Achray,
And fathers wept—those brave old men—
For the ones they might not meet again,
And the little bairns with their lifted hands
At thought of a·home in some distant lands   .
Clung sobbing so with such hopes and fears,
That it filled the bravest eyes with tears.
And men looked on with folded arms,
Who never had felt a home's sweet charms ;
But at times they would glance at the castle gate,
And grasp tneir swords with a frown of hate,
And suppress an oath that grievous morn
With a flashing eye, and a smile of scorn.

Slowly at last through the woods below
The exiles wound on their weary way,
With heavy hearts in their tearful woe,
And little they said that words could say.
But scarcely a league had they left behind
The castle's walls with its banners fair,
Ere they heard like the rush of a mighty wind
The whir of wings in the morning air.
And thousands of birds in a cloud came down
And swarmed like bees by the wayside green ;
And behind as far as the distant town,
The course of the flying birds was seen.
They came and fluttered with wings outspread,
And swung in the branches overhead,
And chirped, and twittered, and led the way
With dainty flights from spray to spray,
In royal purple, and hermit brown,
In scarlet mantle, and golden crown,
They warbled the sweetest songs they knew,
And about the children's pathway flew,
And for many a mile they sang before,
Till they came at last to the convent door.

And years rolled by, but never again
Was heard their music in wood or glen—
And to-day round the castle's crumbling wall,
The hush of silence is over all !

IN THE DAYS OF LONG AGO.

D O you remember, darling mine,
     When of old we roamed together
By the brook that rippled on
Through the foxglove and the heather—
Creamy daisies flecked the meadow,
Sunset skies were all aglow,
And your eyes to mine were lifted
Gladly in that long ago?

Oh, the years that since have faded,
But a rainbow spans them all,
Though the cottage with the woodbine
Has not yet become a hall.
And the garden, where the blossoms
Pink and white in clusters grow,
Is the same as when we wandered
Down the meadows long ago.

Standing at the stile together—
Where we stood in old lang syne,—
Looking down the western hillside,
Do you sorrow, darling mine ?
True, the dear familiar faces
That our fondest visions show,
All are gone—but we shall see them
As we saw them long ago.

Silver gleams among your tresses
Do not change your gentle face,
And the dying glow of sunset
Fills your eyes with tender grace.
Like the full moon fuller growing
As the sun is sinking low,
Is the light that softly lingers
O'er the days of long ago.

Faith uplifts the weary spirit,
All the strife is not in vain,
And our sorrows seem to brighten,
As the sunshine blends with rain.

For across the twilight waters
Gates of pearl are bright as snow—
Listen ! do you hear the voices
That we heard, love, long ago ?

WITCHERY.

AY-Belle, Adrian, and Flo,
    Under my window on the lawn,
Out where the white-starred mignonette,
The rose, the pansy, and violet
Are sweet with dews of the early dawn,
Romp in the sunshine to and fro,
With tossing curls, and cheeks aglow,
Blue-cap, Roseleaf, and Pigeon-feather,
Under my window all together,
May-Belle, Adrian, and Flo !

What are they doing, I want to know
Under the vine-leafed portico,
And out by the trees of the garden walk
With the sunlight flickering under ?
Something marvellous to be told
Unto the bees with their packs of gold,
That stop in their flight to hear them talk,
With a sudden buzz of wonder.

Dancing around the willow tree,
They are the laughing witches three,
May-Belle, Adrian, and Flo—
And the birds sit round in groups of twos,
Waiting to hear some wondrous news
That only the bees and birds will know
In the bright midsummer weather.
And all the place grows strangely still—
And I lean and listen beside the sill,
Till at last the birds break into song,
And I hear the laughter loud and long
Of Blue-cap, Roseleaf, and Pigeon-feather !

AT SUNSET.

REATHE delicate blossoms about the bier,
    Such as she loved in the long ago,
When the roses bloomed, and the birds were here,
And the skies were bright in this world below.

It has grown so dark, since she left my side,
But alas, I know I am growing old ;
And my feeble steps I can scarcely guide,
And somehow the sunshine is bleak and cold.

Here let me rest in this easy chair—
It was her's through many a weary day,
Where she sometimes sat, when the days were fair,
Watching the ships come up the bay.

There is not a rose-bush, or shrub, or tree,
In the garden bowers, now chilled with grief,

That has not some memory, sweet to me,
With its fragrance folded in bud or leaf.

You see that cluster of violets blue ?
They are faded now in their ancient vase—
She was just as youthful at heart as you,
Though you scarce would think it to see her face.

There is not one thing in the homestead old
That has not its charm of the days that were—
The work-box yonder, this curtain's fold,
And that vase of flowers seem part of her.

Full fifty summers and winters gone,
With her sunshine presence through cloud and
    gloom—
Ah me ! it is dark on the dreary lawn,
It is lone—so lone—in the silent room !

You pity me friend, but the end is near—
I have little to hope for, now below—
The Reaper's harvest is well nigh here,
And I wait with patience my time to go.

Full fifty years since the village bells
Rang merrily on our wedding-day—
And through the forest, and down the dells,
How cheerily sang the birds of May !

She seemed the fairest in all the land—
On the village green I can see her yet—
Though the voice is silent, and cold the hand,
She's as fair to me as when first we met !

Not one old friend of my youthful day
Remains of those who were round me then—
With the fleeting years they have passed away,
And entered that country beyond our ken.

My life is crushed like a withered stalk
In the hands of Time, and my strength is past,
But I falter on in my feeble walk,
With the joyful promise of rest at last.

A few more times to the house of prayer,
A few more times to the old church ground,

And the grass will blossom above me there,
And the world forget, and the years roll round.

Ah me ! but at times when I sit alone,
The past comes back with a tender strain,
As of Autumn breezes that faintly moan,
As of waves that murmur a low refrain.

And I seem to wander beside the mill,
Where of old I toiled with such willing hands,
Till the sun sank under the western hill,
And the moon rose over the summer lands.

And often I seem to stroll again
On the village street in the sunset rays
Through the maple-boughs, and along the lane,
By the meadow-brook of our younger days.

And the roses we set by the garden wall
Of our first new home seem strangely near,
And the sweet young face that I oft recall,
And the songs she sang that I sometimes hear.

And children were mine to kiss and hold—
When these weak withered hands were strong—
But alas ! they are dead—and I am old—
And weary and worn, and the days are long !

By yonder path through the forest trees,
At the edge of the brook we loved to rove,
With the clover breath on the summer breeze,
And the merry music of birds above.

But along life's pathway were thorn and flower,
And sometimes the clouds were black with rain,
But we felt that soon through the blinding shower,
The sun would shine in our hearts again.

We fretted not at the ills of life,
And we knew that the past was beyond recall,
Our hearts grew kindlier for the strife,
With patient feeling for one and all.

Our home with the sunshine of peace was filled,
Till the shadow passed the threshold o'er,

And one by one, as the good Lord willed,
Our loved ones crossed to a brighter shore.

But I'm only waiting with trustful heart,
And low bowed head for the call at last ;
But oft to my poor old eyes will start
The tears as I sadly recall the past.

Nay, leave me alone a short half-hour
By the side of her who was once so fair—
Place in her hand the geranium flower,
Smooth back the tresses of silver hair.

ON A PICTURE OF VENICE BY MOON-
LIGHT.

THE music of flute and tambour
Where the southern moonbeams fall,
And the sweet red roses clamber
Over the garden wall !

In the glow of the moonlight tender
O'er its liquid miles of gold,
In her stately pride and splendor,
Sits Venice, revealed of old.

A Venetian throng is boating
On the dark blue waves aglow,
And I hear sweet voices floating
From the twinkling streets below.

Why the black-robed Abbess lingers
On the staircase do you ask,

As she holds with trembling fingers
To her flashing eyes a mask ?

Through the gloom of cypress yonder,
By the marble balustrade,
She sees two lovers wander
Dreamily in the shade.

His bending plume just reaches
Her hair with its one white rose,
But of his impassioned speeches
No word the lips disclose.

And the Abbess leans to listen
Away from the tell-tale moon,
And the hundred lamps that glisten
In the palace's wide saloon.

But I hear the tinkling tambour,
As I stand within this hall,
With its tints of blue and amber,
And that Rubens on the wall.

But I know this picture's meaning,
For it comes in dreams at night,
When softly intervening
Falls a molten-golden light.

In one of their quaint old churches,
At early mass they met,
Where the light bloomed through the porches,
Into rose and violet.

And with passionate dream these lovers,
Stroll through the dark old hall ;
Behind them an Abbess hovers
In shadow from wall to wall.

For his life no prince might barter
An urn of jewels bright—
For the dagger in her garter
Will pierce his heart to-night !

'Tis the bride of yon cavaliero—
And his wedding ring she wears—

But to-morrow will find our hero
At the foot of some secret stairs.

———

Land where the sun reposes,
Bride of a summer sea,
Realm of the languid roses,
Is the picture true of thee?

A NIGHT IN AN OLD ABBEY.

 VERDUROUS lawn with plants and flowers
Set round a square of moated towers—
A winding river where the yews
On either side form avenues
Whose mingled growth of leaf and vine
Is thrilled with sunshine as with wine,
Or chilled with mist of April rains
That glimmer down the leafy lanes—
A ruin quaint whose ancient wall
And porch, and pave, and court and hall
Have echoed to the clanging tread
Of knights in time of Ethelred,
Or clash of wassail-cups upheld`
By royal hands in days of eld,—
A relic of that olden age
Of lord and jester, prince and page—
When barges slid in summer eves,
Red-canopied with silver gleam

Of moonlight through the listless leaves
That overhung the winding stream—
When from the battlemented roofs
The warden leaned to clang of hoofs,
And heard the bell-gate swing ajar
With sound of voices low and far,
As from the chase a courtly train
Wound slowly up the castle lane—
When Saxon battle-axe and lance
In tourney flashed at Carlyel
Or Camelot, or rang perchance
In fight against the infidel—
When faint and sweet were softly heard
The cithern strings in cadence stirred,
With glimpse of dainty sword and plume,
That vanished in the starlit gloom,
Where roses slept in spicy vales
Lulled by the far-voiced nightingales—
When through the Abbey's gate of stone
Sometimes a wax-light cortege shone
With sable pall, and silent tread,
And chanted service of the dead.

Through blue-stained windows glimmered faint
The moonlight on the figures quaint
Of mail-clad knight, and statued saint.

Two knights lay side by side at rest
With coat-of-arms, and royal crest,
And folded hands upon the breast.

No sound the utter silence stirred
Of footstep, or of whispered word,
Only the wailing wind was heard.

But when its voice had died away
A glistening light of fitful ray
Streamed upward where the two knights lay.

In hollow tones resounded through
Each gloomy-vaulted avenue
The words distinctly of the two.

One hoarsely spake : " The deed was done
Returning home at set of sun
From tourney at brave Caerleon.

"I met at tilt for guerdon rare
The boldest of her wooers there
For favor of my lady fair.

" Sir Ethelred my might defied,
Sir Ethelred my right denied,
And by his treachery I died.

" Alas, by consecrated ground
Hard by my castle I was found
With cloven helm, and gaping wound !

What hap befell him—tell me, hast
Thou known of curse to overcast
His path within the fortnight past ? "

Replied the other :   " 'Tis a year
That thy mailed shape has rested here
Upon a deftly-carven bier.

" A sheath of rust encrusts thy blade,
None lately at thy tomb has prayed,
Where I but yesterday was laid.

" Sir Ethelred has won thy bride,
Thy lady fair doth at his side
The fairest in the kingdom ride.

" He never hath a crime confessed,
No curse doth on his movements rest,
His face hath peace of heart expressed.

" He mourned thee as a brother might,
He praised thee for a valiant knight,
And swore thy wrong to do aright."

To this the voice made low reply :
" In vain the dead must question why
Their wrongs should unrequited lie.

" Yet, 'tis the manner of the earth,
Our deeds are soon of little worth,
Our deaths make often cruel mirth.

" Hast yet a wondrous realm explored
Or light of wing as Ariel soared
Beyond the angel's flaming sword ?

Or hast through caverns dim below
Beheld amid a tempest-glow
Shapes of the damned flit to and fro ? "

The iron form in silence lay,
Till with the moon's declining ray,
Its answer sounded far away :

Sleep, utter sleep.—I faintly mind
A faith in something undefined—
All else forgotten.   Death is kind.

With all its train of pains and woes,
A life well rounded to the close
Brings man at last a long repose.

" Great victory a solace brings
To dying ones whose sufferings
A change will work in many things.

" But when the fevered pulse is stilled,
Not wide proclaim of good fulfilled
Can change the plan that nature willed."

" And then ?   What hast thy vision found
In life or death that doth surround,
More welcome than a peace profound ? "

Then fainter still the voice replied :
" I have forgotten—naught beside
The death I wis—*that* doth abide."

DEJECTION.

'VE been where naught but Error gloried
        Over triumphs won,
Have seen man's crimes in splendor storied
    From sun to sun.

I've felt the sorrow of hopes blighted
    With an aching breast,
And like some traveller benighted
    Have sought to rest.

Love turns to tears at Life's bright portal
    And deep shadows cast
A doubt upon the life immortal,
    Ere morn is past.

For Silence sits enthroned supernal
    In the far beyond,

And from the depths of space eternal
    No lips respond.

Old age burns out its poor existence
    When its hour is late,
And frets not with a dull resistance
    At what is fate.

And youth with early aspiration
    Clutches sword and shield,
Not reconciled to such invasion
    Nor prone to yield.

But when it seeks the gentle faces
    That are now no more,
The soul its stumbling steps retraces
    From that closed door.

Does great Pan sleep this Sabbath summer
    With its Autumn haze,
While Nature mourns him—tardy comer
    Of other days?

No longer hears the reed-pipe calling—
    While Echo grieves—
No longer hears the footsteps falling
    Through forest leaves ?

Where still Arcadian summers linger
    Over grove and grot,
The shepherds fain would hear the singer,
    But hear him not.

Mine ears are burdened with false voices,
    And sweet truth has fled,
I call, but naught the heart rejoices,
    For Pan is dead.

And Silence sits enthroned supernal
    In the far beyond,
And from the depths of space eternal
    No lips respond.

OUR BRETON BRIDE.

HIME, chime ye bells on the morning air,
Birds, sing your wildest gladdest lay,
And meadows your sweetest blossoms wear,
For our loved Fifine is to wed to-day !
The fairies swing on the stalks of wheat,
The white-rose wakes, and the foxgloves stir,
And the birds in the garden are crying Sweet,
As she passes by, for their love of her !

Fair, Oh fair is her wedding-gown,
Woven of silk and as white as snow—
Emerald-green is the myrtle crown
That wreathes her hair in its amber glow.—
And the bridal party has gone away,
The boat has sailed from the river pier,
With a flood of light in the tossing spray,
To the boatman's song, and the landsman's cheer !

Oh, sweet young face in the bridal lace
Who now will lead in the village green,
In the merry dance with your faultless grace,
Since you left us to mourn your loss, Fifine ?
With the lilies float, Oh golden boat,
On the river of Time with its sparkling tide,
Ever with joy to the years remote,
With our Breton lad and his bonny bride !

THE BANSHEE.

ITH loosened locks and features wild
A weeping mother clasps her child ;
The father weaves him to and fro,
Acushla, crying in his woe,
As, with the wailing wind and rain,
A sound goes by the window-pane.

The bog-fire flickers in the gloom,
The shadows hover round the room,
The kettle sings a weary song,
The crickets chirp the whole night long,
But darkly down the gusty plain
A shape sweeps past the window-pane.

It comes when moons are pale or red,
From out the valley of the dead,
Its hair is black, its face is white,

Its bright eyes star the shades of night,
And wailing wild a weird refrain
It hurries past the window-pane.

A horseman rides with speed afar,
Black clouds are shrouding moon and star,
The lightning flashes overhead,
And man and horse lie prone and dead.
And at his home the weird refrain
Is hushed beneath the window-pane.

The crouching dog with lifted head,
Is moaning by his master's bed,
The storm is past—the night is still—
The moon is shining on the hill ;
But loved ones wait, and wait in vain,
And listen at the window-pane.

EVENING.

FRESH are the fields with new-mown hay,
The sun is sinking behind the hill,
As I journey homeward at close of day,
Along the lane in the evening still.
Cottage windows across the pond,
Brightly gleam through the woods beyond,
  And low on the breezes rise
The tinkle of bells from pastures green
And over the bars the horses lean
  With welcoming speechful eyes.

Up from the meadows with loaded wain,
The haymakers come with weary tread,
And chanticleer and his feathered train
Are slowly seeking the barnyard shed.
The sunlight fades and from yonder hill
Faintly the far-off whippoorwill

It's lonely sorrow tells,
And from the farm-house portico,
In a sunset dream of long ago,
    I hear the village bells.

And now the bat in uncertain flight
Is swooping under the twilight trees,
As with star-tapers comes slow night
With vesper chantings in the breeze.
And the owl I hear from its leafy bower
Like some lone ghost in some lonesome tower,
    Far over hill and dale,
Where silver shields of the moonlight seem
Upon the sentry oaks to gleam,
    With serried coat-of-mail.

MY LADY SLEEPS.

 MUST bind my lady's hair
With a wreath of eglantere.
Now her face is white as snow,
I must charm and keep it so.
Should she waken at my touch
She would surely marvel much—
Snow-white cheek would turn to red,
Then I'd think my darling dead !

I must cross her lily hands
Ere she wakes, and understands ;
In the waxen fingers lay
Calla-blossoms, and a spray
Of the dainty mignonette.
She is sleeping gently yet—
Should she stir upon the bed,
Then I'd think my darling dead !

I must on her feet to-night
Draw her satin slippers white,
Fold the drapery of lace
In an idle form of grace ;
Turn her face a little—so—
While 'tis yet as white as snow,
Should she move her gentle head,
Then I'd think my darling dead !

ALL IN THE CHRISTMAS-TIDE.

THE hearth is bright—the night is chill—
The chimney breezes moan and die—
The falling snowflakes crowd the sill,
And creaking footsteps hurry by.
The shop-lights glimmer down the street,
Where shivering human creatures grieve—
Gaunt shapes of misery that greet
The passer-by this Christmas eve !

What songs of angels fill their hearts
To quell the tumult of their woe ?
Through glittering squares and crowded marts,
Like Afrit shapes they come and go.
Lone spirits that the world repels,
What joy to them is that bright morn
That ushers in with chiming bells
The day the Prince of Peace was born ?

The day will come with kindly cheer,
And pleasant dreams of olden times,
Glad greetings charm the passing year,
And blithely peal the Christmas chimes.
The yule-log burn with lusty roar,
The holly glitter in the blaze,
While mirth and minstrelsy once more
Revive the merry-making days.

All in the happy Christmas-tide,
When castle walls were loud with song,
When through the royal archways wide,
Wandered a plumed and jewelled throng.
When round the cottage board were quaffed
Huge tankards of the nut-brown ale,
And oft the stout-limbed swineherds laughed
At some blithe Cedric's jocund tale.

All in the happy Christmas-tide—
(How weirdly sounds the wind to-night !)
Through chapel windows branching wide
In purple grandeur falls the light.

I seem to hear the song of peace
Float softly on the snowy air,
And as the blended voices cease,
The low responses to the prayer.

And here to-night I sit and pore
Over a book of ancient time,
A legend quaint of musty lore,
That ripples on in golden rhyme
About a castle Llenwyn hight
Where under rafters bending low,
A tall coifed lady robed in white
Glides slowly neath the mistletoe.

All in the happy Christmas-tide—
Chilled at the sight are lord and dame,
And when that shape did past them glide,
No soul could answer whence it came.
Hushed was the harper's golden thrall,
The dancers shrunk with trembling fear,
And with white lips did watch the hall
Through which they marked it disappear.

The tale goes on.—Long years ago
A princess of the house was wed,
And here beneath the mistletoe,
That night she mourned her lover dead !
And every Yule-tide from the tomb—
(Was that the lattice-screen that stirred ?)
She crosses o'er the banquet room
But sees no face nor utters word.

But when the Gothic hall is passed,
And from the moon twixt panes of gold,
A silver splendor round is cast
On twisted carvings dark and old,
It turns a ghastly face amain,
It lifts a weird and plaintive cry—
(That sound against the window-pane—
Was that the night-wind sweeping by ?)

It lifts a voice of keen despair,
And turns and passes through the hall ;
And moved as by a gust of air
The banners flutter on the wall.

The guests in satin robe and shoon,
And dight with jewels guard the door—
The lights are out—full shines the moon
On terrace, balcony, and floor.

Without a sign the pallid shade
Comes slowly on with noiseless tread,
Till one brave courtier undismayed
Clasps in his arms the sheeted dead !
When lo ! upon the marble pave,
There sank with something like a sigh—
(How wild the winter night winds rave !
And was that sound a human cry ?

I hear it o'er the stormy blast—
'Tis at the door—nay, at the blind—
The snow is gathering thick and fast,
*And bitter is the moaning wind * * **
O cruel fates that drive apace
Of starving creatures such a host—
But here beside the hearth I place
One poor half-frozen shivering ghost !)

THE PASSING SCENE.

HEN the low piping of the birds was heard
At eve, he slept, but wakened with the moon—
Too ill to talk, for days he spake no word,
But now while faintly stirred the airs of June
The curtains by the window, where he lay,
We listened to a voice so passing strange,
We knew at last would come ere break of day,
Revealed in death the sad and solemn change.

We lifted up the pale face in the light,
The cricket's changeless chirping thrilled the air,
And all the plaintive voices of the night
Blended in one sweet symphony of prayer.
We listened to the gentle words he said
Recalling years whereof he seemed to dream,
And hopes and fancies of the dear days fled,
Like withered flowers, on life's lapsing stream.

Again he heard the Sabbath evening bell
Sound sweetly under twilight skies of gold,
Or wandered down the quiet village dell
Below the mill as in glad days of old.
And lifting up his feeble hand the glow
As of some far-off vision filled his eyes,
As if he stood joy-radiant below
The angel-terraced walls of Paradise !

The vision of the dear ones long years dead,
The glory of the dawning after death,
Upon his face a peaceful radiance shed,
While faint and faltering grew his failing breath.
Then to the Holy Book he turned once more,
And while we read the passage that he loved,
He clasped our hands—life's last sad scene was o'er,
And leaning back, he neither spoke nor moved.

WHISPERS OF THE ANGELS.

OMETIMES I think the angels listen
  Unto our little ones here below,
And follow with eyes that tearfully glisten,
Their wandering footsteps to and fro.
And over our households in hamlet or city,
And over the old familiar ways,
There lingers, leaning with look of pity,
Ever the angel of other days.

Ever the presence of those departed—
The little darlings of long ago—
And mothers who mourn and are broken-hearted,
Look up in tears from their depths of woe.
They may not see in the mist before them,
The outstretched arms, or the tender gaze,
But still in their sorrow is bending o'er them
Gently the angels of other days.

You look in the eyes of the loved one left you
And dream of the skies on that fairer shore,
Where one stands waiting since death bereft you,
And cast its shadow across your door.
The past comes back, as with fond caresses,
The little one to your heart you fold,
But the tears will fall in the sunny tresses,
As you mingle your gray hair with the gold.

In the last faint gleams of the embers burning
You sit to-night in the easy chair,
And your heart recalls with a throb of yearning
The little head that was bowed in prayer,
The little hands that were prest together,
Meekly uplifted in homage true,
And you stifle a sob as you wonder whether
Those little arms are outheld for you.

And your thoughts go back to the days of anguish,
To the time when your child grew strangely ill,
When she left her playthings and seemed to languish
With drooping eyes, in your arms so still ;

When she looked so pale on the pillow lying,
With tangled locks, and her poor thin hand
You held in yours, when you thought her dying,
With a glow on her face of a brighter land.

You remember how in those gloomy hours,
With whisper low on her couch of pain,
She longed to look at her garden flowers,
And asked if the roses would come again?
But the days go by, and the silent river
Sweeps on with never a token fond—
But faith is yours, though the black racks quiver,
And cloud the sky, and the stars beyond.

Those weary days—those days of sorrow—
Your lifted hands that were clenched in woe—
Your heart that yearned for that vague to-morrow
To end its agony here below!
And many a night with her long hair gleaming,
She seemed to come to you unawares,
And you heard her footsteps—dreaming—dreaming—
Steal lightly down the crystal stairs.

How lone and drear with its silence lingers
That snowy couch in your memory yet,
How fair she seemed with her waxen fingers
Upon her breast with the mignonette !
'Twas a violet ray from the vase of roses
That fell on her lily-bordered bed,
And she seemed like one who in sleep reposes,
When you lifted the face-cloth of the dead.

There's a little mound in the churchyard yonder
Where the birds are singing the long day through,
And thither in summer hours you wander
With flowers like those she brought to you.
For they all were hers with their tearful faces—
The hooded pansy she called her nun—
The valley lilies in bridal laces,
The daisies that leaned to the summer sun.

And your eyes grow dim as across the meadow
You catch a glimpse of the grove below,
With its rustic arbor, and half in shadow,
The brook where the water-cresses grow.

For often beneath the old oaks swinging
You saw her white form through the trees,
And heard her merry laughter ringing
Sweet and clear on the morning breeze.

How fondly she looked in your eyes when weary
You sat on the porch as the sun went down,
When she drew your face to her own so cheery,
And laughingly kissed away your frown !
Sometime—you whisper with holy feeling—
You will clasp her close, you will hear her speak,
When the shadows lift from the shore, revealing
The angel form of the one you seek.

Nay, weave not thoughts with the funeral garland,
The sombre pall, or the shrouded urn,
In a brighter land than the shining star-land
Is dwelling the darling for whom you yearn.
What of these flowers so brown and faded,
With their ribbon she tied, in her love for you,
Is the heart of the garden, you think, invaded
By the biting thorn, and the bitter rue ?

Is it the touch of a presence holy
That thrills you to-night with a tender grace ?
Or is it the gate that is swinging slowly,
Through which you can see her angel face ?
The moonlight steals through the snow-white cur-
      tain,
And softly falls on your silver hair,
But the doubt has fled, and the hope uncertain
Is changed to faith in your silent prayer.

Be trustful—the angels are ever near you,
Their unseen pinions are rustling by,
They come and go with their smiles to cheer you
In saintly crowds from the silent sky.
Ever descending with love and pity,
To dear ones left on the earthly shore,
Through the pure white gates of the shining city
They pass and repass forevermore.

They come when the morning with touches tender
Awakens the lilies in crowns of white,
And the waves of dawn in their purple splendor
Break into gold on the shores of night.

When the far-off evening bells are ringing,
And a silence falls on the twilight sea,
With voices low are the angels singing,
As they sang by the waters of Galilee.

MYSTERY.

PLEASANT it is these eves to sit
On the wide old porch of the farmhouse here,
While about the roof of the red barn flit
The sidelong swallows twittering near ;
    And across lots a mile away
  Towering over the fir-tree copse
  You can see the tall round chimney-tops
    Of a mansion old and gray.

'Twas a curious structure in days of old—
Nobody lived there—so they said—
But the tale I remember the townsfolk told
Was something of those who were long years dead.
    And each Gothic window and door
  Was grim as the gates of a prison wall,
  And year after year the silent hall
    A gloomy record bore.

Once by the cobwebbed entrance sat
A man in the costume of years ago,
In quaint brass buttons, and broad-rimmed hat,
Who leaned on his staff, with head bent low
          In the shade of the evening there,
And when he lifted a weary face,
Of sorrows many was seen the trace,
          And of age the silver hair.

Over the mansion a spell was thrown—
It seemed like an evil sprites' abode ;
Under the moss-grown stepping stone
The black snake hid, and the spotted toad.
          And when the wind went by,
The shutters uttered a doleful note
Like the sounds that fill a chimney's throat,
          A weird and plaintive cry.

The well was sunken, and over-run
With a tangled growth of weed and flower,
And the bat and owl that shunned the sun
Haunted at night the crumbling tower.—

Out on the grass-grown lawn
I remember the sun-dial stained with rust,
And the fountain urn that was filled with dust,
But the rustic seat is gone.

Long years it has stood neglected—dead—
No hand has striven to break the spell
That clothes it round with fear and dread,
Nor can a soul its history tell,
Or how, or when 'twas built.—
Upon its piazza floor a mark
They say discolored is, and dark,
Where human blood was spilt.

And many a night the village folk
Have seen a pale face through the pane
Or followed a shape in muffled cloak
Till it vanished down the lonely lane
Below the fir-tree copse ;
All day the birds fly in and out,
At dusk the swallows skim about
Those crumbling chimney tops.

No human footsteps are ever heard
Within those lonesome walls of stone,
But ever the attic-blind is stirred
Where ghostly trees make doleful moan—
        And at night through the willows tall,
The moon peers in with tresses white
And seems to rest long arms of light
        Upon the window wall.

A film of dust lies on the floor,
And silently from room to room
Small shadowy footprints glide before
The eye and vanish in the gloom.
        And the staircase deep and wide
Will creak with the sound of unseen feet
And tremble as if some dread *affreet*
        Had sought its depths to hide.

There's a witch whose constant theme is death—
Who tells of a house where blood was shed—
Of drabbled locks, and gasping breath
Of an old man struggling upon his bed,

Where the curtains' tightening band
With its choking folds to his throat is prest
And a blood-stained dagger in his breast
Is clutched by a small white hand !

THE FEAST OF SAN MARCO.

W HY does that eremite sit at the feast,
    With his sharp black eyes, and his tonsured
        hair?
Not jolly is he like that fat old priest,
Or the white-faced notary lean and spare,
With his elbows resting upon the board.
A twinkling eye hath our liege, his grace,
And the young court gallant with tilted sword
Hath a roguish look in his fair young face—
But the devil himself you would almost swear
Leans back in that dark-browed hermit's chair!

His brow is wrinkled, his hand is thin,
As it toys with the goblet of ruddy wine,
So thin that the bones show through the skin
And white as a woman's—I wis as fine
As a high-born cavaliero's hand.

But the night before, in the narrow street,
There swooped from the mountains a robber band,
There were cries of murder—a hurry of feet—
And this black-eyed hermit's hand was red,
From shriving the dying—the good folk said.

A hermit's a hermit—and why should he
In his Capucin cowl, and his priestly gown,
Sit here at the feast, and as lordly be
As the one patrician of all the town
Who can melt his pearls in his wassail-cup ?
Now listen ! I saw him a fortnight since—
This pious recluse who has come to sup—
Through the catacombs guiding our host, the prince.
But what of these candlesticks quaint and old,
And this antique plate, and those cups of gold ?

Above the Cathedral del Parto stands
The home of a sculptor embowered in vines.
Beyond it glimmer green meadow lands,
Before it the far-twinkling water shines
Of the blue bright bay of Naples.   Here,
(Now but a dream of the past, alas !)

Dwelt his daughter Carita, and year by year,
She met with the black-eyed monk at mass.
Then she disappeared—and that hermit there
Was gone for a month and a day—but where?

If you wander by night in this city of ships,
This town with its mountain that shadows the west
Like a huge black giant that sits with its lips
Drooling lambent fire down its rugged breast,
Have a care for your life, for the veriest cur
Can stand in a passage and strike you dead,
And none but a priest might hear a stir
As he passed on his lonely way to bed.
A far faint sound by the dark sea wall,
A splash in the water—and that is all!

But they say of this hermit in Capucin gown,
Who sits at the feast looking solemn as fate,
In this black grim castle just out of the town
So famed for its wine, and its rare old plate,
And its quaint-wrought silver of long ago,
That a man like this they have sometimes seen

In the mountains watching the path below,
Leaning over the rocks with his carabine.—
And that dread volcano ! that red-mouthed hell !
Who knows what secret its depths could tell ?

Did he know this prince in the years ago
Till he met him starving and gave him bread ?
Does he hive in the catacombs down below
In the dark deep vaults of the loathsome dead ?
Where is his hermitage ?   Who can tell ?
And whence came his patron's treasures old ?
Is his chamber of skulls a penance cell,
Or hung with tapestry fringed with gold ?
If they seek it, they'll find it, without a doubt—
But I question their chances of getting out !

AT THE OLD HOME.

" We may build more splendid habitations,
Fill our rooms with paintings and with sculptures,
But we cannot
Buy with gold, the old associations."

Longfellow.

TILL as of old the blue bird sings
  Over the winding woodland walk—
In yonder meadow blithely swings
The bobolink with tipsy wings
Upon the bended mullein-stalk.

I see the old home through the leaves
That twinkle in a maze of gold,
And round its quaint old-fashioned eaves
The woodbine still a mantle weaves
The same as in the days of old.

Here by the brookside path I strayed
In sunny hours when days were long,
And birds the same sweet music made,
Though now from cloistered grove and glade,
There seems to come a sadder song.

The names we carved upon the tree
Have disappeared this many a year ;
And where the old oak used to be,
Only the vision comes to me
Of faces that were then so dear.

A bridge is built across the stream
Where once we placed the stepping-stones ;
I hear the waters now that seem—
Like far-off music in a dream—
To greet me in familiar tones.

Up yonder lane the schoolhouse old
Still stands amid surrounding farms,
And as I now the place behold
What dreams of youth each scene enfold
As with the clasp of loving arms !

The children play upon the green
Light-hearted as in days of yore,
But other faces seem to lean
With tender gaze upon the scene,
Whose step will come again no more !

And yonder is the churchyard keep,
The close within whose sacred fold
Some now in solemn silence sleep,
Above whose graves the pansies peep,
And lilies lift their crowns of gold.

And as the sunset's glory dies
Above yon village spire aglow,
I seem to hear with tearful eyes,
A strain of music from the skies.
And voices of the long ago !

THE CHEYENNE MASSACRE.

IFT up your hands that clutch for gold,
And spurn the heathen from your path:—
His hand is red, his heart is cold,
He well deserves your Christian wrath !
O bid him in his sorrow go,
Take life and land and sate your greed
Of gold though tears and blood should flow,
Then justify your noble deed
By any creed that you may know !

The Indian hath no rights to serve,
Or sense to wrong, or soul to save,
O never from your purpose swerve
But hound the culprit to his grave !
'Tis surely not the Christian way
To take the red-man by the hand—
Lift meek and humble eyes, and pray

For heathen in some other land—
Some creatures on a foreign shore
Who worship God in sun and stars,
Let in the light through golden bars
To them who need your service more !

The Master surely never taught
Compassion for this savage race,
So lift a mild beseeching face
And steal what other men have bought.
Go satisfy a greedy love
Of gain, and slay your fellow-man,
But sanctify the deed above
By God's own teachings if you can !

THE LAST LETTER.

 TAKE it away for it burns my brain,
And my heart is breaking—no light—no
    day—
No love to soften the cruel pain
That my spirit suffers—take it away !
'Tis the last fond letter he wrote when ill,
And could hardly lift his little hand—
And when I found him so white and still,
I cursed the God that had cursed the land !

The words are blurred, and I only see
The large brown eyes, and the poor thin face
So pitiful, waiting and watching for me,
With his arms outheld for a last embrace.
And this letter written with feeble pen
Just as he left it here at his side
To tell me over and over again
How he longed to see me before he died !

How deep the silence that chills the gloom !
No cheery footfall upon the stair,
No gentle voice in the lonely room,
No folded hands at my side in prayer,
Nor the goodnight kiss that my heart has known,
When I clasped him close with a mother's joy—
But only to dream of the past—and alone
To sit and weep for my darling boy !

And I lean at the window—across the way,
On the pavement fronting the busy square,
My little neighbor stops at his play,
And looks at the house with a sober stare.
And I see him sit with his cheek on his hand,
And I know he is thinking of days that are fled,
And vainly striving to understand
What they mean by saying his friend is dead.

And oft when the weary day is done,
And the far-off evening bells sound low,
And through the shutters the sinking sun
Is casting a radiant mellow glow,

I fancy I hear his voice, and seem
To catch his face in the passing crowd,
And I start and wake from a troubled dream,
In the gathering darkness, and cry aloud !

And this is the book—the last he read—
With the leaf turned down at the very page
Where he ceased when weary—and there by his bed,
Is the bird—his bird—in its lonely cage.
But it does not sing with its old delight
When the cheery voice of its friend was heard,
For the room so desolate, once so bright,
Brings a pang of sorrow to that poor bird !

O ever I list to a cry of pain,
And to see through the blinding tears that rise,
The arms that were lifted for me in vain,
And the pale, thin face with the large brown eyes .
And I clasp his letter, and kneeling low,
I pray that the shadow may pass me by,
But 'tis better a thousand times to go—
To fold my hands in my grief—and die !

POTS OF GOLD.

A SLEEPY HOLLOW EPISODE.

" A drowsy, dreamy influence seems to hang over the land, and to pervade the very atmosphere. Some say that the place was bewitched by a high German doctor, during the early days of the settlement; others, that an old Indian chief, the prophet or wizard of his tribe, held his pow-wows there before the country was discovered by Master Hendrick Hudson. Certain it is, the place continues under the sway of some witching power, that holds a spell over the minds of the good people, causing them to walk in a continual reverie. They are given to all kinds of marvellous beliefs; are subject to trances and visions; and frequently see strange sights and hear music and voices in the air. The whole neighborhood abounds in local tales, haunted spots, and twilight superstitions; stars shoot and meteors glare oftener across the valley than in any other part of the country, and the nightmare, with her whole nine fold,seems to make it the favorite scene of her gambols."

The Legend of Sleepy Hollow.

"  RUIN of some ancient hall
   That overlooked the river wall—
A ruin of some old chateau
Built several hundred years ago,
About which ghostly tales are told
Of pirates, who, in days of old,

Along this weird romantic shore
Buried huge chests of gleaming ore."

Thus spake the boatman unto me,
One evening, on the Tappan Zee.

" This ?—why the legend runs that when
Old Hendrick Hudson and his men
Sailed slowly up the river tide,
They saw upon the starboard side
Tall towers, and many-windowed walls,
And heard men shout within the halls,
But when its water-steps were neared,
Enchanted-like, it disappeared ! "

Thus spake the fisherman I met
Intently toiling with his net.

" A fortress of the olden time,
A relic of a golden clime,
When caravels of Spanish seas
Spread sail with treasure-laden hold,

The black flag flying in the breeze,
And manned by swarthy men of old.
Some say, a convent, old and gray,
Where penitents did fast and pray
Three hundred years ago, or more—
For round its ancient Gothic door
Were carven pious legends quaint
Beneath its sculptured patron saint."

Thus spake by Sleepy Hollow's brook
The Dominie with learnéd look.

———

Green leaves were trembling in a maze
Of violet light, and in and out
Tall-towered oaks, the robins flew,
While up each forest avenue,
At times I heard the far-off shout
Of ha! ha! ha! that rose and died
In echoes through the quiet woods.
For all these hazy summer days,
From early dawn to eventide,

POTS OF GOLD.   95

Is Sleepy Hollow's drowsy glen
Still haunted by the little men
In blouses green, and tasselled hoods.
And ho ! ho ! ho ! from every side,
Their voices from the woodland rise
Where willows old, with tresses sleek,
And withered oaks, whose knots are eyes,
Do seem with hollow tone to speak.

From twinkling brook, and bracken dense,
Such summer sounds as lull the sense,
Thrilled the warm air of one fair June
Through all a drowsy afternoon.
I strove to read, but o'er the book
Nodded, and slept beside the brook,
Until a voice above me spoke,
That seemed to issue from the oak,
Whose mantle's shining fret and fold
Shimmered like cloth of green and gold.
For now the moon above the woods
Shone full upon a wondrous scene—
Deep forest glades, and solitudes,

With boulders black that seemed to lean
Over the hills, where softly shone
The cascade-waters of a stream,
Broke on my vision like a dream.
Before me stood with ancient wall,
Arch, bastion, turret, lifted tall,
A huge portcullised pile of stone.
A drawbridge wide was outward thrown
Above a moat, while in the glow
Of moonlight, men walked to and fro,
Along the upper wards, or leant
Over the steep-walled battlement.

But lo ! my very self in sooth
Had suffered change from head to heel.
I wore such garb as men in truth
Once used in days of proud Castile,
When in the reign of Ferdinand,
Its Spanish pirates swept the seas,
Or bandits scoured the mountain land.
Huge leathern hose reached to my knees,
A long knife glittered at my waist,

Beneath a doublet silver-laced,
While near me in the spectral gloom,
A musket lay with hat and plume.

" What vessel sails up yonder bay ? "
I heard a voice ring on the air,
As filled with terror and dismay,
I watched the lights flash here and there
Within that fortress weird and tall.
I crossed the swinging drawbridge where
The lamps streamed from the windowed wall,
Athwart the mellow moonlight air,
And stood within an ancient court
Where loitered men with clanking sword,
Or wildly clashed in boist'rous sport
Their flagons, at the banquet board.

In high-heeled shoes, and doublets red,
With belted steel, and Spanish hat,
And clay-white features like the dead,
They met my gaze and silent sat,
As if rebuking with a stare,

The man who dared to trespass there.
Till one above the ghastly crowd,
Peered 'neath his hand, and cried aloud :
" 'Tis only poor dumb Winkelried
Returned from hunting in the wold,
So get ye fellows hence—make speed
And safely house the pots of gold ! "
At once I strove to speak, but found
My lips refused to utter sound,
And quite as pale of face as they,
Upon a bench beside the door,
I watched the ghostly figures fade
Deep in the shadow of the glade.
The moonlight blue through arches gray,
Gleamed on the forest-skirted shore
Whence lightly came the dip of oar,
While on the bosom of the bay
A full-rigged bark at anchor lay.

The men returned with heavy tread,
Bearing their burdens through the gate—
Their features were as like the dead

As those beneath a coffin-plate.
And from the Gothic underwall,
The spectral glare of torches shone,
Like flambeaux at a funeral
Within some abbey's crypt of stone.
The sound of mattock and of spade,
Broke the dark stillness of the place,
While through the deep rotunda's shade,
At times I saw a pallid face.
Again I heard a murmur low,
That louder grew with every breath,
Then clash of steel, blow after blow,
With curses loud through arches wide,
That echoing back, the walls replied—
And then—a silence deep as death !

———

I woke beside the twilight stream,
In Sleepy Hollow's haunted dell,
And like strange voices in a dream
The waters' murmur rose and fell
Over the rocks beside the mill.

The boatman's song came up the bay,
The fisher's skiff at anchor lay,
While far-off o'er the distant hill,
I faintly heard the village bell.

AT THE CHURCHYARD GATE.

N a perfect moonlight night,
(The warm south breezes flew
Whispering through the leaves,
And I heard the brook sing too
Mournfully, mournfully,
Like the voice of one that grieves)
I saw in the yellow light,.
Come from its churchyard bed,
Clothed in its grave-gown white,
The ghost of my friend long dead.

And its shimmering tangled hair
Down to its feet it shook,
And its wax-white face did wear
Such a wild and piercing look,
That I shrank from its presence there,
With fear, by the moaning brook.

Of the burden of secret tears,
And the anguish of other years—
It spake with a hollow sound,
Under the cypress tall—
Of its bed that was cold and wet,
Of its long night underground,
And the death-damp that lingered yet
On its brow for the past, and all.

" They dug down deep,
And covered me over,
And left me to sleep—
But I heard the clover
Whisper, whisper through the night,
When I started up with fright
At the footsteps of my lover.

' Why does he seek me dead,
And weep above my mound ?
His tears come down, and I stir in bed,
Wake in my cold bed underground,
And rise, and seek him where,

· On the garden seat, in the pale moonshine,
Of old he smoothed my shining hair,
And pressed his lips to mine.

"But he sees me not, nor lingers
  A moment, nor does he know,
As I clasp in my thin cold fingers
  His hands, that I love him so.
I kneel at his side to cheer him,
  In the gloaming and the dawn,
But when he feels me near him,
  He rises—and is gone.
    The night grows old,—
    Oh, the earth is cold
  Under the cypress tall—
    But to-morrow, to-morrow
  For the sinning and the sorrow
He shall know all!"

AN INCIDENT OF THE AUSTRIAN REVIEW.

IFT up the golden tassels,
  Let the floss run through your hands—
In the sunlight how it glistens
  With its broad and purple bands !
No lordlier bridle ever
  Was worn with coat-of-mail
In the days of old with Arthur,
  Or glorious Percivale !

Softly the silver music
  Steals through the palace gate,
And without, the Austrian standards
  And the royal guardsmen wait.
To-day victorious heroes
  In the grand review will ride,
Whom the Emperor and Empress
  Will greet with royal pride.

His majesty's steed is waiting,
  And he mounts, and the champing line
Moves out to the hills beyond them,
  Where the steel-bright squadrons shine.
And the Empress in her carriage,
  As it halts for the grand review,
Is hailed with huzzas of homage
  From loyal hearts and true.

With nodding plumes and banners,
  And with flying eagles gay,
Now legion after legion
  Sweeps by in proud array ;
Chasseurs with lance and guidon
  Pass on with prancing tread,
And tattered flags are lifted
  That veteran heroes led.

And across the shining levels,
  The mounted squadrons wheel,
And with lances lifted proudly,
  They gleam long lines of steel.

Then like a gathered storm-cloud,
They thunder down the plain,
When from the watching thousands,
Goes up a cry of pain !

For a little child has wandered,
And stands demure and still,
In the pathway of the troopers,
As they swiftly round the hill.
Then its little arms are lifted,
As they touch the level plain,
And with tottering feet it reaches
To the shouting crowds in vain !

When behold, a stalwart horseman
Drops his lance, and swinging round,
O'er his charger's neck, in safety
Lifts the maiden from the ground !
Ten thousand ringing bravos
For the hero and the man—
And the little one is riding
With the foremost in the van !

Soon back the trooper gallops
With the little child before,
And halts and yields the darling
To a mother's arms once more.
And joyfully the Empress
Is smiling through her tears,
And again the hills re-echo
With the loud and ringing cheers !

Dismounted, stood the soldier
At the Emperor's command,
While all the army wondered
As he clasped the hero's hand.
With the proudest badge of valor
The trooper's breast he starred,
And bade him mount his charger
As the captain of the guard !

Lift up the golden tassels,
Let the floss run through your hands—
In the sunlight how it glistens
With its broad and purple bands !

No lordlier bridle ever
Was worn with coat-of-mail,
In the days of old with Arthur,
Or glorious Percivale !

A MIDSUMMER DAY'S DREAM.

ITH eyes ashine in the summer sun,
   A squirrel peeps through the branches down,
And over their gossamer bridges run
The spiders in jackets of blue and brown.
And here in the grass under fleecy skies,
Alone by the marge of the prattling brook,
With a wonderful light in her big brown eyes,
Sits a fairy reading a fairy book.

Across the way by an ancient oak,
An ouph is weaving a magic screen,
In bent-grass feather, and sun-bright cloak
He sits a glimmer of gold and green.
The curious birds stand just aloof,
And timidly gather about the place,
And watch him toiling on warp and woof,
But flutter back when he lifts his face.

Two by two from the mountain wall,
Winding down through the drowsy glen,
Two by two through the poplars tall,
Are filing the troops of little men.
And hark to the music far away,
The singing of merry elves and trolls
Comes like the linnet's moonlight lay
Over the mossy woodland knolls !

In plumes, and jewels, and tasselled hoods,
In pea-green doublets, from groves and lawns,
Elves that toil in the cool green woods,
With pointed ears like the dancing fauns,
White-beard gnomes that guard the gold,
And hide the diamond from mortal sight,
Light-winged fay, and goblin old,
Laughing pixie, and water-sprite !

Through a narrow passage and dark as night,
They pass and their forms are hid from view,
And still they follow with footsteps light,
To a tinkling melody, two and two.

Down through the glistening under-walls,
Where lifts a city its turret and dome,
They journey on through the mystic halls
To the summer land of the fairy's home.

When first the throbbings of life begin
In the earth, and the frost escapes the sun,
The wee folk silently sit and spin,
And weave and wind till their task is done.
They toil at the roots of the ancient oak,
They fill with juices the secret cells,
And millions of mattocks with silent stroke
Loosen the ice of the crystal wells.

Through fibrous depths of the leafless trees
With tiny buckets they come and go,
Till the full leaves bow to the bending breeze
And the ripe fruits burden the branches low.
Down shining ladders of sun and rain,
They bear full measures of warmth and cheer,
To mountain, and meadow, and fertile plain,
Through golden months of the passing year.

But the story ended abruptly there—
A blue bird up in the old oak tree,
Is pouring forth on the drowsy air,
A jubilant melody wild and free.
And a spider is running across the book,
And a squirrel looks down with mute surprise,
And here by the marge of the prattling brook,
A fairy is rubbing her big brown eyes!

AT LAST.

OU will fold your hands,
    While fond ones weep,
And with weary eyes
Will go to sleep
    At last—
Thinking perhaps of the morrow
    Or the years now past.

But the morning after,
When the light draws near,
Will your thought go back
To the old days here,
    Now past ?—
We will not know in our sorrow,
But we shall at last—
    At last !

ON THE CAMPUS.

NO faces now, that erst were known
    Along the gray old seat of stone,
But figures weird, and gaunt and old,
Rise strangely up and frowning fade
Before me through the cloistered shade.
By arch, and corridor, and gate,
Strange faces grow from out the gloom
That once passed by in solemn state,
Now long years buried in the tomb.
Here Horace seems to loiter by,
Half love, half satire in his eye,
With old Anacreon, whose lyre
Love ripples in its golden strings,
Faints with the ardor of his fire,
And dies among its echoings.
There Sappho, ever fair and young,
Plucks with low eyes some fancy sweet

That coyly hides itself among
The tufted grasses at her feet.
While yonder stretched upon the green,
An old white-bearded man is seen
With anxious face, and troubled look,
Scanning the pages of a book.
Beside him on his elbow propped
Another form its book has dropped,
And from the lips the smoke-wreaths rise
And skyward lead the dreamy eyes.
The first then turning grave and slow
With accents neither high nor low,
But in the middle voice, exclaimed:

"O bard by seven cities claimed,
It aches itself my weary head,
To find out what I really said
Though once I wrote it plain. Can you
Tell me the thought *you* had in view
In ' bridge of battles ? ' Was it ' bridge '
Or did you truly write it ' ridge ? '
Bold metaphors I ween must needs

Be used to chronicle bold deeds,
When Hector's plume exultant seeks
Encounter with our father Greeks,
Or Ajax bids his friends deploy
Along the windy plains of Troy."

The bard shook out his long white hair,
And said :

" I little know, or care
What Scalliger or Poppo wrote—
You'll find it all in Anthon's note.
Euripides, take my advice
I'm Homer, lucid and concise.
For centuries I groaned and grew
Distracted more and more like you.
Whenever I was certain quite
Of what I'd truly meant to write,
Some new edition would come out
And plunge me deeper into doubt—
And so Euripides, I say
Let commentators have their way.

They've learned their trade, these men and know it.
They want no guidance from the poet ;
And if you wish to read your plays
With easy mind, these summer days,
Drop Leipsic texts, my trusty crony,
And do as I do—use a pony.
That's what I've learned.—And that is why
I'm blowing smoke-wreaths to the sky."

Thus with full heart revisiting
The halls where hope and friendship grew,
Though Time may still his triumphs bring,
This moral still I sadly drew—
Whatever braver poets sing,
The old is better than the new !

AN ANGEL'S FLIGHT.

HREE shadows pass across the moon
The solemn night is strangely still,
The heart-throbs of the sleeping June,
Do all the soul of beauty thrill.
Three angels—on each brow a star—
High heaven's arch are flying through,
But one speeds downward peering far
Across the crystal depths of blue.

Within a cottage lies the dead,
Upon the face a starry glow—
Tread softly ! for the spirit fled
Scarcely a moment's time ago.—
A fair-haired boy stands at the pane,
And sees a star sweep down the sky—
' *Mamma is coming back again* "—
I heard the little darling cry.

WHAT IS LIFE?

(INSPIRED BY THE TEACHINGS OF ZAMBRI THE PARSEE.)

AID the Poet folding his filmy wings
　"Life is the song that my loved one sings !"

" Evolution is Life to the uttermost age ! "
Said the Scientist growling and bristling with rage.

" It is *Vita !* "—the erudite Scholar replied,
As he gnawed on a Chaldaic root at his side.

Which the queer Antiquarian met with a laugh,
As he showed his white teeth at an old epitaph.

" My friends,"—the Philosopher croaked from a
　tree,
" 'Tis a frightful disease !—we are symptoms,"—
　said he.

" Pooh-pooh ! "—hissed the Doctor uncoiling for
strife,

" When *we* remove symptoms, what then pray, is
life ? "

" 'Tis a thistle "—the Warrior sententiously brayed,
" Something pleasant to take "—and he searched for
a blade.

" All wrong ! "—cawed the Lawyer—" To live is To
be ! "
And he opened his bill for the usual fee.

" Life "—chattered the Sage—" why, of course,
protoplasm ! "
And curling his tail round a branch, had a spasm.

The Nonagenarian trumpeted loud
That Life was a cradle, some dust, and a shroud !

THE INQUISITION.

BENEATH huge granite walls,
In the heart of the Appenines,
Where the sunlight never falls,
And the moonlight never shines,
Where the howl of the wolf is heard
In the depths of the forest trees,
But never the song of bird
Is borne on the morning breeze,
With its gates of triple locks,
And its iron-windowed wall,
Black-ribbed in the mighty rocks,
Stands the Inquisition Hall.

Like fires from Vulcan's forge
That flash through smoky skies,
From the gates on cliff and gorge,
A red light leaps and dies.

From a chamber grim and black,
Through the windows barred with steel,
Comes a cry from the creaking rack,
And a groan from the turning wheel,
As men with a hurried tread,
Are tightening belt and brace,
And Death from an iron bed
Looks up with a ghastly face !

The cruel monk Felician
In sable gown and hood,
At the Court of the Inquisition
Before his victim stood.
And the hot and angry glow,
From the furnace flames below,
Through that chamber black and old,
Fell full on the captive there,
With eyes upturned in prayer,
And a look of calm submission
On his features white and cold.

Only another martyr
For his heresy to bleed,

Who had spurned with scorn to barter
His conscience for a creed !
Fill up the flaming cresset,
With cruel heart and cold,
And with blood-stained fingers bless it
In the tenets that ye hold !
O sombre-browed confessors,
Did thus the Master do
That ye dare to judge transgressors
By the laws that govern you ?

Before them firm and fearless
Francisco Carro stands,
With features pale and tearless,
To hear the Court's commands.
Shadowed in gloom behind him,
The torturers in black,
Await with ropes to bind him
To the malefactor's rack.
But ere the judge had spoken,
Out stood the victim there,
With voice subdued and broken,
Half defiance, half despair :

" Most potent worthies hear me—
Ye to whom monarchs bow—
But think not that I fear ye
Or seek your pardon now !
Where the peaceful moonlight glistens
By the shores to me so dear,
There's one to-night that listens
For a voice she will not hear.
There's one who weeping lingers
By an anxious mother's knee,
And clasps her pleading fingers
In prayerful love for me.
And behold upon the morrow,
In your torture-hall in state,
Ye will care not for the sorrow
Of that widowed mother's fate.
But mark me, haughty master,
This heart will not deny
Its faith, nor stern disaster
Declare its life a lie !
Did thus the Holy Teacher
Reveal His gentle life,

That ye crush your fellow-creature
In your bigotry and strife?"

Around that deep rotunda,
Sat men in grim attire,
Who heard his words with wonder,
Whose hearts were filled with ire.
But one whose teeth in anger
Were set with tiger-hate—
As the chains with deafening clangor
Rang down the prison gate—
Strode forth, a mighty giant,
And the man's assumption cursed,
Who spurned him back, defiant,
And bade them do their worst!

Now fiercely those around him
Had hurled the victim back,
And with lightning speed had bound him
At a signal to the rack.
And with cruel torture straightway
The huge weights slowly fell,

While flickering flames crept nearer,
With a bluish glare and clearer,
When, from the distant gateway,
Loud clanged the castle bell !

At once the grim Confession
Had stayed the massive wheel,
As through the spectral arches
In stately order marches
A Capuchin procession
From the Convent of Castile.
But scarcely had it entered
The weird and lurid glare,
Ere round its chief it centred,
With a strange and solemn air.
Aside they flung their vesture,
And in that lurid gloom,
Men stood with threatening gesture,
In helmet and in plume !

Swift in their places shifted,
The massive bars slid back,
And a senseless form was lifted

From the torture of the rack.
And one with features rigid,
Kneeling with quickened breath
Above that figure frigid
In the chill embrace of death,
Upraised his blade before him,
And swore upon its cross,
By the sainted one who bore him,
To avenge a brother's loss !
Then to the chief Felician,
He crossed the castle floor,
And bade his Inquisition
Fling wide each dungeon door!

Stout men-at-arms obeyed him
And the inner gates swung back,
To a scene whose sight dismayed him
In those hollow walls and black.
No stubborn creed or error
In penance might atone
For the cold and nameless terror
That chilled those walls of stone.

For in the cells before them,
Were shapes in ghastly crowds,
With the pall of darkness o'er them,
And clad in iron shrouds !

Then spake the brave Castilian
To the cowled confessors there,
While shadows fled affrighted,
As the gloomy halls were lighted :—
" Though your council awes the million
There are men ye cannot dare !
Your fate behold before ye
Your crimes may man forget—
Doomed to the fate ye cherish
For others, thus ye perish
And these walls shall crumble o'er ye,
Ere another sun shall set !
For thus O mighty brothers
Ye taught the lesson true,
To do what unto others
Ye would have them do for you ! "

From the prison-walled Confession,
From the Abbot's stern abode,
That night a grim procession
Wound down the mountain road.
And where the moonlight drifted
Above them through the trees,
A cloud of smoke was lifted
And borne upon the breeze.
And lo, where flames ascending
In wrath did writhe and toss
Like stormy hosts contending—
Was the shadow of a cross !

EGLANTINE.

A H me ! so many years ago,
It seemeth like a dream of mine—
My little one with cheeks aglow,
Merrily dancing to and fro,
Through shade, and shine, and eglantine—
Ah me ! so many years ago,
It seemeth but a dream of mine !

It seemeth but a dream to me,
With all the birds about the door,
And leafy glimpse of rock and tree,
And laughter ringing cheerily,
As in the happy days of yore ;
It seemeth but a dream to me,
With all the birds about the door.

The winsome pansy tipt its hood
Of purple, through the creeping vine,

And slanting through the leafy wood
A swaying, golden ladder stood
Of shade, and shine, and eglantine,
And sweet the dreamy solitude,
And drowsy shade of beech and pine !

But now the house so sad and still
Is old, and falling to decay—
The forest path, the droning mill,
The spring where oft we drank our fill,
Together, many a summer day,
No longer now with pleasure thrill,
But like a dream have passed away.

But yonder through the twinkling trees,
Where stands the forest gray and old,
'Twixt mountain skies, and forest seas,
Is swaying lightly in the breeze,
A shifting ladder's bridge of gold ;
And through the mist the birds and bees
Fly in and out the forest old.

And sometimes when the day is done,
And evening skies are all aglow,
Far up the bridge of mist and sun,
I seem to hear my angel one
In accents singing sweet and low,
As, ere her life was scarce begun
I heard her sing so long ago !

INDIAN SUMMER.

NOW come the Indian-summer days
　　When violet colors fill the seas,
When ghostly horsemen storm the trees
With fibrous banners, and a haze
Of gold high-walls the hollow hills.
When goblets brimmed with sparkling dew
Are poised by elves, and to the rills
The sprites and warlocks bid adieu.
When airy cradles swing in pines
Dew-spangled through the pendent vines ;
When haunted ruins, gray and old,
Are mellowed in a mist of gold,
When o'er the crumbling walls grotesque
The vines are wrought in arabesque,
And through the woods the quiet eves
The footfalls sound in crush of leaves ;
When tented witches warm the wine

That thrills the air with joy divine,
And silence dreams to whispers low
Of some sweet days of long ago,
When yellow bees sang down the thyme
Their burden of a summer clime ;
And from the meadows hot and dry,
Was heard the twang of harvest-fly,
And gossip of the bubbling brooks ;
And elbow deep in sunny nooks,
You read a page, in quiet dale,
Of some serene Arabian tale.

VERS DE SOCIÉTÉ

(*Face p.* 134.)

A FOREST IDYL.

BLANCHE. MABEL.

Blanche.

THIS is the spot, beneath these shady beeches
Close by the lake we'll here our luncheon
spread,
The blue waves glistening on the sandy reaches,
The forest thrilled with bird-songs overhead.

Mabel.

Here in the shade we'll dine in sweet seclusion ;
And then a glorious sail upon the lake—
How nice it is away from man's intrusion,
To be one's self and some true comfort take !

Blanche.

There's Aubrey Vane how much he'd like to share it,
Our proud Hyperion with his lofty air—
This cake's delicious with crushed ice and claret,
So far away from dusty Burnham Square.

O here to sit beneath beech-branches spreading
Their cool shade with the sunlight flickering down—
You know the Vernons are to have a wedding
Sometime next Autumn at their house in town ?

Mabel.

Why yes, they've been engaged a year and over,
They met last season at the Springs, one day—
The groom-to-be is really such a rover—
But quite attentive to his *fiancée.*

And such a grand trousseau I hear is ordered,
The dress a satin with a *princesse* skirt,
Three yards of trail with snow-white roses bor-
    dered—
Just think, dear Blanche, and Fannie such a flirt !

Blanche.

I know, and who'd have thought that she would
    marry
When last we met at Narragansett Pier,
But all the girls were there in love with Harry—
Behold this chow-chow—what a feast is here !

Mable.

Indeed, in wedding handsome Harry Percy
I think that Fan at last has found her mate,
He's rich, and talented, and handsome—*Mercy!*
There goes a spider right across my plate !

Blanche.

I wonder where Ned Varden is—

Mabel.

Out boating—
I heard him say last night he'd try an oar.

Blanche.

Then possibly he may be near us floating—
We'd better go more inland from the shore.

Mabel.

How tiresome are their hum-drum conversations
At Germans, kettledrums and masquerades,
Compared with those how sweet the recreations
Here in the forest's deep delightful glades !

Blanche.

With nature's glorious temple o'er us bending,
With drifts of music floating o'er the lake,

Sweet voice of birds and surge of waters blend-
    ing—
O heaven preserve us !—there's a horrid snake !

Mabel.

Where shall we go?—we cannot leave our hamper ı
Here in the woods with bugs and snakes, O dear !
What if it rains?—a most unpleasant damper
'Twould be upon our jolly banquet here !

Blanche.

How dark it grows above the thick horizon—
O, from this rock there's such a splendid view—
The grandest sight that ever you laid eyes on,
See how those white-caps lift above the blue !

Mabel.

Come, let us go to some retreat that's safer,—
Dear me ! I wish we'd asked them, after all ;   ı
They both had really no excuse to stay for,
We hinted that there might come up a squall !

Blanche.

No, no, dear Mabel—we would only quarrel,
Ned Varden is so strangely over-nice,

We'd have to pucker up our lips with sorrel,
And look demure, and be as still as mice.

Mabel.

No swinging on the overhanging branches—

Blanche.

No romping through the knee-deep clover then—

Mabel.

But Mabels prim, and sober-minded Blanches,
To wait upon two vain, conceited men.

Blanche.

Is that a boat upon the lake I wonder?
'Tis but a speck upon the water—hark !
I thought I heard a distant peal of thunder—
The sky is surely growing very dark !

Mabel.

What shall we do ?

Blanche.

Hie to some mansion spacious,
I see a house through yonder forest glade—

Mabel.

Quick then, and gather up the dishes—Gracious !
A pinch-bug's crawling in the marmalade !

Blanche.

O this is dreadful !—what with fun and frolic
And feast enough for half-a-dozen beaux,
Not one of them with any taste bucolic
But really might have joined us if he chose.

Mabel.

We hinted that we might expect their presence,
But O the men are blind as bats, you know—

Blanche.

If they were here, they'd rather hunt for pheas-
ants,
Than on the lake to have a quiet row.

Mabel.

There comes the rain !—I'm sure I felt it sprinkle,
We'll both be drenched ere shelter can be had—
The storm will drive us like poor Rip Van Winkle
Into the mountains thin and poorly clad !

Blanche.

Ye fauns and satyrs what a lonesome dinner
Ye revel over in your wild domain !—
But look dear Mabel !—sure as I'm a sinner
There's Ned and Aubrey coming down the lane !

REVERIE.

SHIMMER of satins and pearls
A rustle of silk in the hall—
And I wait for the dearest of girls
Attired for the Charity Ball.
I watch for her coming and sigh,
As she runs with a radiant face,
To kiss her old father goodbye,
In her glory of jewels and lace.

The moonlight shines bright on the lawn,
The carriage awaits at the door,
A slam—and my lady is gone,
And the hurry and worry are o'er.
Ah me ! what a change since the day
Of Sir Roger of goodly repute,
When we danced in the old-fashioned way,
To the music of fiddle and flute.

How the rafters all echoed with fun !
Aye ! those were the days of romance—
And bless me ! how courtly each one
Was in times when to dance meant to dance.
Jenny Lind too was then all the rage,
Castle Garden with lights was ablaze—
'Twas really a musical age,
And what music there was in those days !

When concerts were famous of song,
And Mario's voice was divine,
When rapt was the listening throng
In singing enchantingly fine.
Old ballads, old customs, and friends—
What fond recollections are stirred,
What glory of sentiment blends
With the songs that no longer are heard !

How well I remember the night
Of the famous Hungarian ball—
When of beauty and fashion the sight
Was a wonderful one at the hall.

And well I remember the pain
It gave me to pick up a fan—
In my tight-fitting coat I was vain—
Too vain—for a corpulent man !

And now at reception or fête,
What changes the fashions reveal,
Money-musk is to-day out of date,
And the grand old Virginia Reel ;
The Tempest no longer is known,
Speed the Plough is a thing of the past—
I declare how the seasons have flown
Since we danced the old favorites last !

I lounge in my library chair,
While the flickering embers go out—
As I cannot myself, I'm aware,
Laid up as I am with the gout.
But like foam of the champagne *rosé*
Old memories sparkle to-night,
And there lingers a fragrant bouquet
Of the days that were filled with delight.

MY PIPE AND I.

SOME REFLECTIONS IN THE CHIMNEY-CORNER.

OLD pipe, gray-headed and serene,
Thou Friar Tuck of ancient glory,
What realms together we have seen,
What lands explored of pleasant story !
And if thy cheek be somewhat scarred,
And that poor nose of thine be broken,
Thy jolly face, albeit marred,
Is still of royal cheer a token.
Together by the drowsy glare
Of winter faggots blithely burning,
We've conned such lessons here and there,
As surely might be worth the learning.

We've seen men enter glad of heart
Aladdin's halls with lamps enchanted,
Have watched them silently depart

Full oft without a favor granted ;
Have learned that piety to pass
Must needs be clothed in goodly raiment
To worship well, each soul, alas !
Must stand its share of ready payment.
Have found that men are wiser far,
Who strive to make each other better,
And seen how eager creatures are
To draw a sword, or forge a fetter.

We've learned that murder is a crime
If poverty stands in the docket,
But that the law will yield in time
To him who pleads with well filled pocket.
When at our doors the dying moan
Is heard from lips of starving sinners,
We pray the Lord in doleful tone
To bless our own abundant dinners.
And while our cities teem with those
Whose rags betoken sad conditions,
Without a stint the money goes
By thousands to the Foreign Missions.

We know that for some purpose strange
There still exists the scandal-monger,
Doomed for a certain time to range
The country through to sate his hunger,
That churches oft are marts of trade,
With games of chance at times the fashion,
That men care not how money's made
While cheating is the ruling passion.
That folks pretend to be devout
And church dissensions strive to kindle,
That others pray in church and out
While plotting some infernal swindle.

We've found that those we trusted most
Who seemed at heart such true believers,
Have proved to be a sorry host
Of robbers, knaves, and base deceivers.
We've learned that bigotry and cant
Have each an influence pernicious,
That fashions grow extravagant,
And men become more avaricious ;
That nothing ever can be done

To change the knowledge of the knowing—
And that we care not—neither one—
Old pipe you're out—and I am going.

FLIRTATION.

" Ah, when the thick night flares with drooping torches,
Ah, when the crush-room empties of the swarm,
Pleasant the hand that in the gusty porches
Light as a snowflake settles on your arm."

Dobson.

COUSIN GEORGE.—COUSIN CLARA.—THE COUNT.—

THE MARQUISE.

I.

Clara.

ET us to yonder arbor go
 Away from the glare of the chandelier,
Where to the music sweet and low,
I will tell you about the Count, my dear.

George.

No, here in the shrubbery, just us two,
Where the moonlight falls through the trailing vine ;

I'm tired of dancing,—aren't you ?
We'll discuss our friends o'er the cake and wine.

Clara, (absently).

But isn't he splendid ?—such heavenly eyes !
And the badge he wears—for his rank you know—
A ribbon with brilliants of gorgeous size,
That the Emperor gave him long ago.

George.

O yes, I remember—but tell me, love,
Were you vexed thus coldly to pass me by,
On his arm—

Clara.

Why, what are you thinking of ?
'Twas a trifle rude, I will not deny,
But I was enchanted, *sans pensées,*
By the glowing language in which he told
Of his home in Italy, where they say
His cellars are filled with heaps of gold !

George.

Heaps of rubbish !—for a louis d'or,

He'd mortgage his all—and a woman's hand
He'd gladly exchange his title for
Did it place a bank-book at his command.

Clara.

He wouldn't !

George.

He would !

Clara.

Hush, George, my dear,
A nobleman's honor is quite *piqué*
And should he happen to overhear—

George.

He could turn his head the other way.

Clara.

I wouldn't be jealous !

George.

Miss Stubborn I'm not—
But people will talk—they know we're engaged—

Clara.

But surely Sir Spiteful it isn't the spot
In which like a bear to become enraged.

George.

I simply ask you not to betray
Such a strange predilection for Count Chalieu
With his beautiful eyes, (he squints by the way,)
And his wonderful badge ; (wears corsets too !)

Clara.

I wouldn't be foolish if I were you.

George.

O, do as you please—

Clara.

I would have you know
That I'm not quite yet a tyrant's slave,
To nod at his beck, or to do so, so,
Or to bend at his feet and his pardon crave.
Obey his orders, now here, now there,
To plead for a smile, to receive a frown,
And to hear him state with a pompous air

That he wants his slippers and dressing-gown ;
To fill up his horrid old meerschaum—faugh !
And if one should chat with a former beau
In the street, on the drive, at the opera—pshaw !
She wouldn't pay for it—O no—no !

George.

Clara, you wrong me in talking so—
My honor, dear girl, I shall always hold
Above reproach, and you ought to know
That it cannot be flimsily bought and sold,
The favor I asked you was surely small,
But I will not press it—no matter how
You have made me suffer—

Clara.

     After the ball
I will talk to you dear, but I cannot now—
You are easily hurt—and had better go
And bask in some silly woman's glance,
Who will be to your taste quite *comme il faut ;*
But *now* I'm engaged for the coming dance.

II.

(An hour later—The Count and Clara on the veranda overlooking a moonlit terrace.)

The Count.

'Tis a charming night—it would almost seem
Like the dreamy nights 'neath a Southern moon,
Where the twinkling lamps on the waters gleam,
As you look from the porch on the wide lagoon,
And hear the voice of the boatmen call,
Or the chanted song to the dipping oar,
While the moonbeams down through the arches fall
In snow-white drifts on the palace floor.

Clara, (deeply interested).

Beautiful Venice !

(After a pause.)

Do you know I dream
Of its mystic nights, and its sunset days,
Of its tinkling lutes, and the doves that seem
On the church of St. Mark to sound its praise ?
Of its balconies hung with cloth-of-gold—

The Count.

Shy looks at mass with its artless maids—

Clara.

Its winding galleries dim and old—

The Count.

Moonlight flirtations, and serenades—

Clara.

And O the sea—the beautiful sea !
With its flash of sail in the Western sun—
When the doves fly home, and the revelry
And the masquerade is but just begun !

The Count.

And stars like lilies upon the breast
Of the slumbering waters rise and fall,
And happy the woman—thrice happy and blest—
Who can look from the porch of her palace hall,
And know that its grandeur is all her own,
That Venice is hers with its lion and dove,
As it lordly sits on its granite throne
With its swirl of waters and songs of love.

Clara.

To a Southern maid it would be sublime
Whose home was Italy—

The Count.

True, indeed !
And I fancy the maid of another clime
Would like the picture—

Clara.

She might not lead
A lonelier life on an Afric shore
In the horrid hut of an Ashantee
If that Southern life should yield no more
Than a palace beside a romantic sea.

The Count.

But what if love should attend her there ?

Clara, (reflectingly).

Oh, some might like it—and—some might not—
Love turns bleak walls to a marble glare
In a frontier lodge, or a sea-side cot—
Rough stones into pavements polished fine—

Wild vines into curtains of rich brocade,
Or damask in all its golden shine—
But (*wearily*)
   —better than all is a rich old maid !

The Count.

In the coldest of hearts love kindles its flame—
Behold the Marquise in the garden here
On the arm of a lover—she said the same,
But she wedded her husband within a year,
And survives the Marquis now three years dead.
Has a castle at Pau—vast acres of land—
And a fortune immense in Spain 'tis said—

Clara, (intently peering over the balcony).

('Tis George, as I live—and—he clasps her hand !
O why did I leave him ? what *did* I say—)

The Count, (continuing).

Reputed a grandee's daughter too—
'Tis love at first sight—ah, well-a-day !
Life is full of romance—

Clara, (nervously tapping the floor with her foot).

I listen to you—
But I fear I am not—

The Count, (starting up).

You are pale you are faint—

Clara.

It is nothing at all—you were going to tell—
(Oh dear ! it's enough to provoke a saint !)
Let us seek the *salon.*   I am not—quite well.

III.

(*On the garden terrace by the fountain,   George and
the Marquise.*)

The Marquise, (presenting a rose).

Will you wear this, *mon ami*, a white moss rose,
And remember the meaning it has for you,
That under its leaves you will not disclose
What I tell you ?—then listen.   She's truly true—
But somewhat capricious, as all girls are ;

She fancies you jealous I think, and so,
She loves to carry perhaps too far
A little flirtation—

George.

But then, do you know
This proud Chevalier in his thin gauze mask,
Whose palace in *fact* is a castle in Spain,
A Utopian villa—

The Marquise.

Pray, why do you ask?—
I think you are now in a cynical vein—
You cannot refer to the Count Chalieu
Whose *fêtes* are so splendid on St. Mark's eve
At his palace in Venice? Of course I do!

George.

The stories about him do *you* believe?

The Marquise, (laughing.)

Why, I knew the count in the days of old,
Then a Monto Christo he seemed to be—

Whatever he touched he turned to gold,
And he owned vast lands and had ships at sea.

George, (dubiously).

Then he *is* a count ?

The Marquise.

A fact—'tis true.

George.

Has a palace in Venice ?

The Marquise.

He has indeed.

George.

Of servants a lordly retinue ?

The Marquise.

More than a princely house might need.

George.

I'm surprised at this—

The Marquise.

Why didn't you know
He's a Chevalier of the Golden Cross—

In the Pyrenees has a fine château—
In business schemes never met with loss—
And travels for pleasure ?—come let's stroll
On the moon-lit terrace—the night is warm
And I know that waltz would enchant your soul
Did not some fair one possess the charm.
Now am I not right ? (*looking up into his face.*)
    But I somehow fear
That you love another—

George.

    That could not be.

The Marquise.

You think she is still to your heart so dear ?

George, (abruptly).

Why, what do you mean ?

The Marquise.

    Oh, it seems to me
That your heart might meet in the "madding crowd"
Some other whose fealty you could not doubt.

George, (indignantly).
Of her truth and devotion I'm justly proud
But I pray you Madam—

The Marquise, (coaxingly).
Let us not fall out—
I was only in jest—we must still be friends—
I see her sweet face through the vines above,
Pray seek her thither and make amends,
I was only testing your strength of love.

    (*Leaves him at the staircase of the veranda.*)

George.

(*Meeting Clara pale and agitated, leaning against one
of the pillars of the conservatory.*)

I left you engaged for the dance, my dear—
Are you ill—

Clara, (interrupting him).
I have sent for my carriage, sir—

George.
And where, O where is your cavalier?

Clara.

If you mean the Count, he is seeking *her*
La grande Marquise whom you flatter so
With such tender grace, and whose rose you wear—

George.

I'm surprised indeed that you do not know—

Clara, (with a hint of tears).

Whose husband they say was a millionaire,
Great nabob prince in some distant land,
Who owned a palace across the sea—
But I know it all—you would seek her hand
For the wealth it brings, and be false to me!

George.

Are *you* aware they are friends indeed—
The Count and the Lady—but neither knows
That the other deceives—both friends in need.
And love each other, as such love goes?
But you know too well that I could not forget
The love that I bear you, if hope were dead.

Clara.

And did I offend you when last we met,
And do you forgive me the words I said?

George.

Let all be forgotten—'twas I that erred—
Let me hold your shawl—your carriage is here—

Clara, (in the moonlight).

Oh, you are so rude!—

* * * * *

(*Whispering*)—but just one word—
I'll expect you to-morrow at tea, my dear!

A WATERING-PLACE IDYL.

" So far beneath your soft and tender breeding."
                                              Twelfth Night.

ELL here we are at last in clover,
    Far from the city's dust and din ;
I thank my stars the journey's over
That I did dread so to begin !—
Who was it on the front veranda,
That smiled so sweetly when you met ?
Was that young Buckingham, Amanda ?—
Why he was never in our set !

Too bad we didn't reach the races—
But O this noon, 'twas scorching hot !
I wonder if we'll meet old faces,
Or find them all a horrid lot !
I heard it said Goodhopes was winner—
That horse on which Matilda bet—

The Lloyds are here—they're now at dinner—
But they were never in our set !

There goes the Stuyvesant's new carriage—
Just come from France the other day—
Was that Miss Paul ?—again her marriage
Has been postponed a year, they say.
Am sorry—but she is so fickle—
And he's in such an awful pet !
The Pauls were always in a pickle—
I'm glad that *they're* not in our set !

The Bluchers always spend the season
At some old farm-house out of reach—
Indeed for quite as good a reason,
The Puffers go to Brighton Beach.
I do declare !—why Mr. Hermanns !
'Tis such an age since last we met—
And all last winter at the Germans,
We did so miss you in our set !

Yes—we remain until September,
If so ordain the kindly fates—

The Duncans?—Oh, I do remember—
I think they're stopping at the States.
Good bye—now dear without appearing
Too rude—I say it with regret—
Fred Hermanns is so hard of hearing,
We can't endure him in our set!

You know his sister Lily married
The Marquis Cheatamseaux at Rome—
But only with his lordship tarried
A fortnight ere she sailed for home.
He couldn't prove—and so they parted—
His title to a coronet—
The girl was almost broken-hearted—
You know she wasn't in our set!

I wonder if Miss Vane is coming—
Our Boston friend of bookish lore,—
So fond of Kant, and always humming
An aria from some classic score.
Here come the Lanes, with horses prancing,
And liveried footmen black as jet;

They never dance—though fond of dancing—
Unless in our exclusive set !

And Britain's princess—what a pity !—
Can't come till August, if at all—
We'll have to journey to the city
To match our satins for the ball.
You know in dress, without exception,
There'll be such rigid etiquette !
Of course 'twill be a grand reception,
And quite *en règle* with our set !

It's growing dark—the band is playing—
The shop-lights twinkle down the street—
O dear !—I fear, as I was saying,
That few have come we care to meet !
Hand me my fan—this heat is torrid—
It's hardly time to worry yet—
But wouldn't it be downright horrid
Not to meet any of our set ?

TO A COQUETTE.

YOU remember when last we were boating
On the beautiful river below,
How sweet was our flirting and floating
Together, a long time ago ?
Where the lindens the avenue shaded
You remember returning to tea,
When the light of the sunset had faded
You said you were tired of me?

I thought you were charming and pretty,
When afterward, down at the train
I hoped you would stay in the city
And not come to see us again.
But the summers were bright with your beauty,
You came every June to the place :
I told you (in penance of duty)
I hated the sight of your face !

My sister you thought so romantic,
Her love was so tender and true ;
But me you deemed slow and pedantic,
From sonnets I'd written to you.
You remember the mill in the meadow,
That stood where the blue river ran ?
It was there that we sat in its shadow,
And the fun of your flirting began.

I read to you charming romances,
The piano with fantasies rang ;
You thrilled me with sweetest of glances,
And laughed at a song that I sang.
I met you again in the city,
You called me your villager beau—
I ventured to say you were witty,
You ventured to tell me to go.

I remember the lover that met you,
One evening below in the dell ;
You left me abruptly—I let you—
I couldn't do otherwise, well.
I gave you a book, and some flowers,

You took them, and threw them aside ;
I know you don't think of those hours,
So thoughtless you are in your pride.

One night as the rain fell in torrents,
We parted—I held to my heart—
And journeyed to Paris and Florence,
And Rome with its treasures of art.
I took neither trinket nor token,
To trouble my memory here ;
I found that my heart was unbroken,
And wondered you ever were dear.

Returning I find you unmarried,
Your beauty's the same, I am told—
For suitors you always have carried
A heart that is icy and cold.
But come to the Beeches to-morrow—
We're leading the gladdest of lives ;
I'm over my sickness and sorrow,
And will show you the sweetest of wives !

WEST POINT.

Satins and laces and beautiful faces."

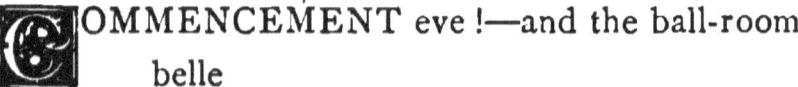OMMENCEMENT eve !—and the ball-room
        belle
In her dazzling beauty was mine that night,
As the music dreamily rose and fell,
And the waltzers whirled in a blaze of light.
I can see them now in the moonbeam's glance
Across the street on a billowy floor,
That rises and falls with the merry dance,
To a music that floats in my heart once more.

A long half-hour in the twilight leaves
Of the shrubbery—she with coquettish face,
And dainty arms in their flowing sleeves,
A dream of satins, and love, and lace.
In the splendor there of her queenly smile,

Through her two bright eyes I could see the glow
Of cathedral windows, as up the aisle,
We marched to a music's ebb and flow.

All in a dream of Commencement eve—
I remember I awkwardly buttoned a glove
On the dainty arm in its flowing sleeve,
With a broken sentence of hope and love.
But the jewels that flashed in her wavy hair,
And the beauty that shone in her faultless face,
Are all I recall, as I struggled there
A poor gray fly in a web of lace.

Yet a laughing, coquettish face I see,
As the moonlight falls on the pavement gray,
And I hear her laugh in the melody
Of the waltz's music across the way,
And I kept the glove, so dainty and small
That I stole as she sipped her lemonade,
'Till I packed it away I think with all
Of those traps I lost on our Northern raid.

But I never can list to that waltz divine
With its golden measure of joy and pain,
But it brings like the flavor of some old wine
To my heart the warmth of the past again.
A short flirtation—that's all, you know—
Some faded flowers,—a silken tress—
Her letters I burned up years ago
When I heard from her last in the Wilderness.

I suppose could she see I am maimed and old,
It would soften the scorn that was changed to hate
When I chose the bars of the gray and gold,
And followed the South to its bitter fate.
But here's to the lads of the Northern blue,
And here's to the boys of the Southern gray,
And I would that the Northern Star but knew
How the Southern cross is borne to-day !

www.ingramcontent.com/pod-product-compliance
Lightning Source LLC
Chambersburg PA
CBHW022356020726

47500CB00002B/305